Billy's Picture

Billy's Picture

by

Margret & H. A. Rey

Houghton Mifflin Company
Boston

"I want to draw a picture,"
said Billy the Bunny.

So he took a pencil and began to draw.
Just then Penny the Puppy happened to
come along.

"That's a pretty picture," said Penny. "But it needs a HEAD. Please let me do it." And he took the pencil and drew a head with long floppy ears just like his own.

"There you are," he said. "That's the way
it should be." "But. . . ." Billy began.
Just then Greta the Goose happened to
come along.

"That's a lovely picture," said Greta.
"But it needs FEET. Please let me do them."
And she took the pencil and drew a pair of
feet just like her own.

"There you are," she said. "That's the
way it should be." "But what. . . ." Billy began. Just then Paul the Porcupine happened
to come along.

"That's a wonderful picture," said Paul. "But it needs QUILLS. Please let me do them." And he took the pencil and drew lots and lots of quills just like his own.

"There you are," he said. "That's the way
it should be." "But what I. . . ." Billy began.
Just then Ronny the Rooster happened to
come along.

"That's a beautiful picture," said Ronny.
"But it needs a COMB. Please let me do it."
And he took the pencil and drew a comb
just like his own.

"There you are," he said. "That's the way it should be." "But what I wanted...." Billy began. Just then Oliver the Owl happened to come along.

"That's a great picture," said Oliver. "But it needs WINGS. Please let me do them." And he took the pencil and drew a pair of wings just like his own.

"There you are," he said. "That's the way it should be." "But what I wanted to. . . ." Billy began. Just then Maggie the Mouse happened to come along.

"That's a sweet picture," said Maggie.
"But it needs a TAIL. Please let me do it."
And she took the pencil and drew a tail just
like her own.

"There you are," she said. "That's the way it should be." "But what I wanted to draw...." Billy began.

Just then Eric the Elephant happened to come along. "That's a delightful picture," said Eric. "But it needs a TRUNK. Please let me do it."

And he took the pencil and drew a trunk
just like his own. "There you are," he said.
"That's the way it should be."

"But what I wanted to draw." Billy began once more —and this time nobody happened to come along—"what I wanted to draw isn't a PUPPYGOOSE or a PORCUPHANT or whatever you call this silly picture. All I wanted to draw was a picture of myself!"

Here Billy began to cry and for a moment nobody said anything. Then everybody started to talk at the same time.

"A picture of myself— that's just what I wanted to do!" said Penny and Greta and Paul and Ronny and Oliver and Eric.

Billy stopped crying. "Why not do it then?" he said.

And that's what they did: Eric drew an
elephant and Maggie drew a mouse. Paul
drew a porcupine and Greta drew a goose.

Penny drew a puppy and Oliver drew an owl. Ronny drew a rooster—and can you guess what Billy drew?

That's what he drew!